This edition published in 1990 by Gallery Books,
an imprint of W. H. Smith Publishers, Inc.,
112 Madison Avenue, New York, NY 10016.

Gallery Books are available for bulk purchase for sales
promotions and premium use. For details write or telephone
Manager of Special Sales, W. H. Smith Publishers, Inc.,
112 Madison Avenue, New York, NY 10016. (212) 532-6600

ISBN 0-8317-42674

Printed in Hong Kong

CHICKEN LITTLE
and LITTLE HALF CHICK

PICTURES BY BERTA AND ELMER HADER

GALLERY BOOKS

CHICKEN-LITTLE

CHICKEN-LITTLE went into the wood one day, and an acorn fell upon her head.

"Goodness me!" said Chicken-Little, "the sky is falling. I must go and tell the King."

So she went along and she went along and she went along until she met Henny-Penny.

"Where are you going, Chicken-Little?" asked Henny-Penny.

"Oh," said Chicken-Little, "the sky is falling and I am going to tell the King."

"How do you know?" asked Henny-Penny.

"I saw it, I heard it, and part of it fell on my poor head," said Chicken-Little.

"May I go with you, Chicken-Little?" asked Henny-Penny.

"Certainly," said Chicken-Little.

So they went along and they went along and they went along until they met Cocky-Locky.

"Where are you going, Chicken-Little and Henny-Penny?" asked Cocky-Locky.

"Oh," said Henny-Penny, "the sky is falling, and we are going to tell the King. Chicken-Little saw it and heard it and part of it fell on her poor head."

"May I go with you?" asked Cocky-Locky.

"Certainly," said Chicken-Little and Henny-Penny.

So all three of them went to tell the King that the sky was falling: Chicken-Little, Henny-Penny, and Cocky-Locky.

They went along and they went along and they went along until they met Ducky-Lucky.

"Where are you going, Chicken-Little, Henny-Penny, and Cocky-Locky?" asked Ducky-Lucky.

"Oh," said Cocky-Locky, "the sky is falling and we are going to tell the King. Chicken-Little saw it and heard it and part of it fell on her poor head."

"May I go with you?" asked Ducky-Lucky.

"Certainly," said Chicken-Little, Henny-Penny, and Cocky-Locky.

So all four of them went to tell the King that the sky was falling: Chicken-Little, Henny-Penny, Cocky-Locky, and Ducky-Lucky.

They went along and they went along and they went along until they met Goosey-Poosey.

"Where are you going, Chicken-Little, Henny-Penny, Cocky-Locky, and Ducky-Lucky?" asked Goosey-Poosey.

"Oh," said Ducky-Lucky, "the sky is falling and we are going to tell the King. Chicken-Little saw it and heard it and part of it fell on her poor head."

"May I go with you?" asked Goosey-Poosey.

"Certainly," said Chicken-Little, Henny-Penny, Cocky-Locky, and Ducky-Lucky.

So all five of them went to tell the King that the sky was falling: Chicken-Little, Henny-Penny, Cocky-Locky, Ducky-Lucky, and Goosey-Poosey.

They went along and they went along and they went along until they met Turkey-Lurkey.

"Where are you going, Chicken-Little, Henny-Penny, Cocky-Lockey, Ducky-Lucky, and Goosey-Poosey?" asked Turkey-Lurkey.

"Oh," said Goosey-Poosey, "the sky is falling and we are going to tell the King. Chicken-Little saw it and heard it and part of it fell on her poor head."

"May I go with you?" asked Turkey-Lurkey.

"Certainly," said Chicken-Little, Henny-Penny, Cocky-Locky, Ducky-Lucky, and Goosey-Poosey.

So all six of them went to tell the King that the sky was falling: Chicken-Little, Henny-Penny, Cocky-Locky, Ducky-Lucky, Goosey-Poosey, and Turkey-Lurkey.

They went along and they went along and they went along until they met a Fox.

"Good day to you," said the Fox. "Where are you going in such haste, Chicken-Little, Henny-Penny, Cocky-Locky, Ducky-Lucky, Goosey-Poosey, and Turkey-Lurkey?"

"Oh," said Turkey-Lurkey, "the sky is falling and we are going to tell the King. Chicken-Little saw it and heard it and part of it fell on her poor head."

"Come along with me," said the Fox, "and I will show you a short way to the King's palace."

So they all followed the Fox: Chicken-Little, Henny-Penny, Cocky-Locky, Ducky-Lucky, Goosey-Poosey, and Turkey-Lurkey.

They went along and they went along and they went alo
lived with her hungry little cubs. In they went after the Fox.
And to this day no one has told the King that the sky was

until they reached the underground hole where the Fox
d they never came out again.
ng.

LITTLE HALF CHICK

ONCE upon a time a Spanish hen hatched out some nice little chickens.

One, two, three came out plump and fluffy; but when the fourth shell broke, out came a little half chick! He had only one leg and one wing and one eye!

As soon as he could walk, little Half Chick showed the most naughty ways, worse than any of his brothers.

He would not mind, and he would go wherever he wished. He walked with a funny little hoppity kick, hoppity kick, and got along pretty fast.

One day little Half Chick said, "Mother, I am going to Madrid to see the King! Good by."

The poor hen did everything she could think of to keep him from doing so foolish a thing. But little Half Chick laughed at her in a naughty way.

"I am going to see the King," he said. "This life is too quiet for me." And away he went, hoppity kick, hoppity kick, over the fields.

When he had gone a little way, little Half Chick came to a little brook. The brook was in much trouble.

"Little Half Chick," whispered the water, "I am so choked with these weeds that I cannot move. I am almost lost for want of room. Please push the sticks and weeds away with your bill and help me."

"The idea!" said little Half Chick. "I cannot be bothered with you. I am going to Madrid to see the King!"

Then he went away, hoppity kick, hoppity kick.

A little farther on, Half Chick came to a fire, which was choked with damp sticks and was in great trouble.

"Oh, little Half Chick," said the fire, "you are just in time to save me. I am almost dead for want of air. Fan me a little with your wing, I beg."

"The idea!" said little Half Chick. "I cannot be bothered with you. I am off to Madrid to see the King!" And off he went laughing, hoppity kick, hoppity kick.

He had hoppity kicked a good way, and was near Madrid. Then he came to a clump of bushes, where the wind was caught fast. The wind was in great trouble, and begged to be set free.

"Little Half Chick," said the wind, "you are just in time to help me.

"Please brush aside these twigs and leaves. I cannot get my breath. Help me quickly!"

"Oh, the idea!" said little Half Chick. "I have no time to bother with you. I am going to Madrid to see the King." And he went off hoppity kick, hoppity kick, leaving the wind to smother.

After a while he came to Madrid and to the palace of the King.

Hoppity kick, hoppity kick, little Half Chick skipped past the man at the gate. Hoppity kick, hoppity kick, he crossed the yard.

But as he was passing the windows of the kitchen, the cook looked out and saw him.

"The very thing for the King's dinner!" she said. "I need a chicken!" And she seized little Half Chick by his one wing. Then she threw him into a kettle of water on the fire.

The water came over little Half Chick's feathers. It came into his eye, over his head. It was terrible, terrible.

Then little Half Chick cried out, "Water, don't drown me! Stay down, don't come so high!"

But the water said, "Little Half Chick, little Half Chick, when I was in trouble, you would not help me." And the water came higher than ever.

Now the water grew warm, hot, hotter, terribly hot. Little Half Chick cried out, "Do not burn so hot, Fire! You are burning me to death! Stop!"

But the fire said, "Little Half Chick, little Half Chick, when I was in trouble, you would not help me." And the fire burned hotter than ever.

Just as little Half Chick thought he must die, the cook took the cover off, to look at the dinner.

"Dear me," she said, "this chicken is good for nothing. It is burned to a cinder."

Then she picked little Half Chick by his one leg and threw him out of the window.

He was caught by the wind and taken up higher than the trees.

Around and around he was twirled till he was so dizzy he thought he must die.

"Don't blow me so, Wind," he cried. "Let me down!"

"Little Half Chick, little Half Chick," said the wind, "when I was in trouble, you would not help me." And the wind blew him up to the top of the steeple. There it stuck him, fast!

And there he stands to this day, with his one eye, his one wing, and his one leg.

He cannot hoppity kick any more. But he turns slowly around when the wind blows; and he always keeps his head toward it.